DISASTER STRIKES

Volcano Blast

DON'T MISS A MINUTE OF THESE HEART-STOPPING ADVENTURES!

Earthquake Shock

Tornado Alley

Blizzard Night

Volcano Blast

Volcano Blast

by MARLANE KENNEDY

illustrated by
ERWIN MADRID

SCHOLASTIC INC.

For my in-laws, Jack and Sue Kennedy, who took their children on many wilderness adventures and who continue to share their love of nature and the wonders of the great outdoors with their grandchildren and great-grandchildren.

ISBN 978-0-545-53047-7

12 11 10 9 8 7 6 5 4 3 2 15 16 17 18 19 20/0

Printed in the U.S.A. 40
First printing, March 2015

Designed by Nina Goffi

CHAPTER 1

The remote Alaskan island looked like the setting of a horror novel. Seriously, it was like some monster had swallowed everyone, leaving an empty shell of a town. Ten-year-old Noah Burton swore he hadn't seen a soul since he and his family landed on the island and picked up their rental car — a dented, rusty old truck with an extended cab. From the back seat he shared with his twin sister,

Emma, Noah stared out the window at a single plastic bag floating on the wind down an otherwise still street. Icy fingers of cold seeped in, making it seem all the more dismal. But Grandma Tilda didn't seem to notice. She hummed a happy tune from the front seat, next to his father, oblivious to the creepy surroundings.

"After all the planning, I can't believe we're finally here!" Dr. Burton said.

"Well, we are, Dad!" Emma laughed.

Noah shook his head. How could his family be so cheerful about this weird vacant town, especially since they'd be calling it home for the next twelve months?

Sure, the sky's the same blue as it was in Hawaii yesterday, Noah thought. *And, yes, it's still mid-June and the sun is shining just as brightly*. But what Noah saw out the truck window could only be described as eerie.

The island had once held a busy military base, but it had been abandoned and shut down years ago. Empty office buildings and derelict duplexes lined the streets.

"This place looks like it should be full of zombies," Noah said. "It's practically apocalyptic."

"Oh, I think it's quite quaint. And we're surrounded by such beautiful, breathtaking wilderness!" Grandma Tilda said.

"I can't wait to go bird-watching here," Emma practically chirped as she bounced in her seat. "I heard there are bald eagles, red-faced cormorants, and tufted puffins . . ."

"So what? There are birds in Hawaii," Noah said.

"But not *these* birds. These are birds I've never seen before." Noah caught Emma rolling her eyes at him through her dark blue glasses.

Though Emma was his twin, they looked nothing alike. Noah didn't need glasses for one thing. And for another, he was tall and sturdy, with wavy, copper-tinged brown hair, while Emma was thin and petite, with super straight strawberry-blonde locks.

"But there is, like, nobody here," Noah said.

"I would hardly call three hundred people nobody," replied Dr. Burton.

Noah could tell by his father's voice that he was smiling. That he thought Noah was being silly. This only annoyed Noah even more.

"Besides," Dr. Burton added, "I told you our new neighbors have a boy your age — Alex Kozloff. Remember?"

Noah didn't answer his father. He continued staring vacantly out the window. Alex Kozloff. The kid's name reminded Noah of Boris Karloff, the actor who played

Frankenstein's monster in the old black-and-white movies. Alex was probably just as lifeless and grim as the monster. Which would fit right in to this spooky half-deserted town.

Noah already found himself desperately missing his best friend, Keoni. Just two days ago the two of them were surfing the waves in Hawaii and hanging out on the white-sand beach. Now Keoni and the beach were almost three thousand miles away.

Noah turned his attention to the horizon, where a mountain rose up from a nearby island. This one was completely uninhabited, marked by alternating patches of lush green forest and barren brown wilderness. The mountain emitted a puff of smoke at its snow-tipped summit. It was an active volcano, one of many on Alaska's Aleutian Islands, and it was the reason they would be living in this desolate place. Noah glared at it.

Noah's father was a scientist who studied volcanoes — a volcanologist. Until recently, Noah thought his father had the best job in the world. Dr. Burton had worked at the Hawaiian Volcano Observatory for the past eight years. They'd moved to Hawaii with their grandmother when he and Emma were two, right after their mother died. Noah was so young he never remembered living anywhere else. Hawaii was home.

Dr. Burton's office had overlooked the exciting displays of Mount Kilauea. Tourists came from all over the world to see the showy orange molten lava spray out of the volcano's mouth and ooze down its slopes in glowing, steamy trails. Kilauea was an active shield volcano, but it was also stable and predictable.

But now his father was taking a leave of absence to study a different kind of volcano so he could write a stupid book about it. Emma wanted to be either a naturalist or a volcanologist like their dad, so of course she was excited about the whole move.

Noah wanted to be a professional surfer. Or baseball player. He was good at both. And he had plenty of opportunities to practice his skills in Hawaii. But not here. The water was too frigid for surfing, and even if there were enough kids for a baseball team, who would they play? There was only one school on the island — with about twenty students total.

Noah continued to shoot angry looks at the volcano. The wimpy puffs of smoke it burped looked way more boring than Mount Kilauea's flashy eruptions. Big deal. Where was the fiery lava?

His father had explained he wanted to do research on a stratovolcano, like Mount St. Helens in Washington. When Mount St. Helens erupted, the fallout was spectacular and devastating. But Dr. Burton said it could be hundreds, maybe even thousands of years before this one in Alaska blew its stack. Nobody really knew.

Noah sighed loudly.

"It's only going to be a year," his father said. "We'll have a big adventure here in Alaska and then, before you know it, we'll be back in Hawaii. It's not the end of the world."

But a year seemed like an eternity to Noah.

Dr. Burton pulled into the driveway of a plain tan duplex. "Here we are. Home sweet home," he said.

It did not look sweet to Noah. Home had bright perfumy flowers. It had trees bursting with coconuts and papayas and bananas.

He jumped out of the truck. *Brrrrr!* It didn't feel like home either. He was used to eighty degree weather. Here it was fifty and windy. In June! "This stinks," Noah muttered under his breath.

All at once, the ground rumbled under his feet. Was the volcano scolding him for his insulting thoughts? Noah gave a startled yelp, but as quickly as they began, the vibrations stopped.

"What the heck was that?" Noah asked, his eyes wide.

Dr. Burton laughed. "Just the volcano welcoming us!" He shrugged like it was no big deal. "Actually, small tremors are pretty

ordinary here. After all, there are more than forty volcanoes around these islands. Sometimes they just need to release some pent-up energy."

Noah guessed he could relate. They'd just spent hours and hours getting here, and now he just wanted to run around, scream, thrash his arms in the air, and go crazy. But there were heavy suitcases to lug in and unpack.

Dr. Burton stared at the looming volcano in the distance. "But it is interesting. Tremors in this area are supposed to be so tiny you usually can't even feel them."

Noah couldn't tell if his father seemed excited or concerned by what had just happened. He himself felt spooked. And strangely superstitious, too. He glanced back at the smoking volcano and forced a weak smile of apology. If dismissing it had insulted its pride, he might as well make amends. Just in case.

CHAPTER 2

The next day Noah was greeted by gloomy fog. The family had spent most of the previous day unpacking and organizing. Today, however, they were supposed to take a boat trip over to the volcano so his father could scout the area, take some photos, and set up some of his equipment. But with the fog, the trip didn't look very promising.

The Kozloffs were supposed to stop by soon with the boat keys. Mr. Kozloff was a commercial fisherman who had a large fishing vessel and a smaller recreational boat that Noah's father would be renting. Mr. Kozloff had work to attend to, but the plan was for his son, Alex, to take them over to the volcano since he knew the best placc to drop anchor and go ashore. Grandma Tilda was going to stay behind so Mrs. Kozloff could show her around town and introduce her to some of the people in the community.

The doorbell rang and Noah jumped, even though he knew to expect company.

"Time to meet the Kozloffs," Dr. Burton said, grinning.

Noah winced, thinking once again of Boris Karloff.

But when his father opened the door, Noah was surprised to find that his new neighbors didn't look like grotesque monsters. In fact, the boy reminded him a lot of his friend Keoni from home. Like Keoni, Alex was stocky, with warm, tanned skin and dark hair that matched his eyes. He also had a huge smile lighting up his face.

If I was stuck living on an island with only a few kids, I'd be thrilled to see someone new, too, Noah thought. He suddenly felt a little sorry for the kid.

Introductions were made and Mr. Kozloff assured Dr. Burton the fog would burn off and the boat trip could proceed as

planned. "It's almost always foggy in the morning. Sometimes it sticks around and rains, but it should be nice today."

"That's good news. I'm eager to get started," Noah's father said. "I guess I might as well head for the dock soon, familiarize myself with the boat, and load some of my equipment onto it while we wait for the fog to lift."

"Well, I'm leaving you in terrific hands. Alex knows the boat well and will be an excellent guide. He's gone over to the smaller island with me many times." With that, Mr. Kozloff handed over the boat keys to Dr. Burton and excused himself.

"Are you guys coming to check out the volcano, too?" Alex asked Noah and Emma.

They both nodded.

He gave them the once-over and frowned. "Wearing that?"

Noah and Emma had on T-shirts, jeans, and sneakers — the normal hiking gear they wore to explore the groomed public trails around Kilauea. Alex had on knee-high rubber boots, a sweatshirt, and a navy-blue jacket.

"You guys do have boots and coats, don't you?" Alex asked. "There aren't any trails where we're headed. It's wet and boggy. Sometimes you'll step into the ground and sink halfway up to your knees."

"Yes, that's good advice," Noah's father said. "I was planning on gearing up for the elements. You guys should, too."

Wonderful, Noah thought. *What fun. Traipsing through muck*. But he went ahead and changed anyway. Roughing it in the wild sounded better than spending the day with Mrs. Kozloff and Grandma Tilda, puttering around what amounted to a ghost town.

It was clear and sunny by the time the powerboat was skimming the choppy waves toward the volcano. The Kozloffs' boat was a twenty-two footer with a small cabin. Since it was chilly, the kids stayed inside while Dr. Burton manned the wheel.

Alex and Emma seemed to hit it off right away, both talking in loud voices over the motor of the boat. But Noah didn't feel like making small talk. He wasn't in the mood. He kept thinking that if he were back in Hawaii he'd be soaking up the sun, a surfboard tucked under his arm, sand sticking to his feet. Keoni would be at his side, cracking some funny joke.

Noah heard Keoni's name float into his ear. "Can you believe it?" Emma asked Alex. "When Keoni heard we were moving to Alaska he asked if we'd be living in an igloo. Isn't that ridiculous?"

"He was just kidding around," Noah defended his friend.

"No, he was serious. I had to set him straight. I had to tell him that only Canadian Inuits had igloos. Alaskan Inuits mostly lived in sod huts and skin tents. But that was a long time ago. Everyone lives in regular houses now."

Emma was such a smarty-pants. That came in handy when Noah needed help with homework, but right now her braininess was rubbing him the wrong way.

But Alex just grinned, and Noah studied the boy's friendly face for a moment. "Are you Inuit?" Noah blurted.

Emma kicked him like he said something wrong. But Noah didn't mean to be rude. He was just curious.

"No. I'm native Aleut, actually. There's a difference. Though, I guess we do share many similarities."

"Why do you have a Russian-sounding last name, then?" Noah asked.

Emma frowned and shook her head, which Noah ignored.

"A couple hundred years ago the Aleuts came into contact with Russian explorers and missionaries," Alex explained. "Many ended up adopting Russian last names."

"Oh, I see." Noah nodded and smiled, warming to Alex a bit. He shot Emma a smug look. The kid didn't seem to mind his nosy questions.

After an hour's trip, Alex guided them to his usual landing spot on the shoreline of the island and they dropped anchor. Dr. Burton told the kids they could go exploring for a bit while he scoped out a place to set up his equipment and take soil samples. "Just stay together and meet me back here in three hours," he said. "I brought a packed cooler, so we can eat lunch before we head back. But take a few bottles of water with you in case you get thirsty. And don't get lost!"

"No need to worry," Alex said. "There are plenty of landmarks in this area to guide us, plus I always carry a compass with me."

Emma grabbed three water bottles and tossed them into her polka-dotted backpack alongside her bird-watching book, a journal, and her camera. The kids took off their life vests and hopped out of the boat onto a rocky outcropping. Beyond the rocks they saw mossy green vegetation that led to a black rutted slope where lava had flowed long, long ago.

During the boat ride, Noah vaguely remembered Emma bombarding Alex with questions about all of the birds she couldn't wait to see, and now her new friend offered something Noah knew she wouldn't be able to resist. "Want to go see a bald eagle's nest?"

Of course Emma was all for it, and Noah couldn't bring himself to spoil things for her. It wasn't like he had better things to do.

"Did you know that Hawaii is the only state in America that doesn't have bald eagles?" Emma asked Alex. "Not a single one! I've never seen one in the wild before!"

The twins followed Alex as he picked his way up a gently sloping hill that led to the steeper incline of the volcano. The ground had been rocky by the shoreline, but now it was damp and mucky, and Noah was grateful Alex had warned them to wear boots.

After a while, they passed a small opening in the side of the mountain. It looked like a simple crack, but there was a darkness beyond the split that suggested more. Noah stopped and stuck his head inside to take a look.

"Hey, guys! Look! It's a little cave!" he called out.

"Yeah. There are a lot of those around here," Alex said.

"Noah, stop fooling around!" Emma urged impatiently. "I want to reach the eagle's nest and spend some time there before we have to head back!"

Noah thought the small cave was sort of cool, but he shrugged and caught up to the other two.

The three continued their uphill climb, and by the time they were starting to breathe heavily, they'd arrived. "Over there." Alex pointed. "Hey, the eggs have hatched!"

A patch of sticks gathered in a large circle sat at the edge of a small cliff. Emma spotted two fuzzy gray chicks. Suddenly the mama, with her wide wingspan and noble white head, swooped in and landed next to the little ones.

"This is incredible!" Emma said as she ripped open her backpack in search of her camera.

Even Noah had to admit it was a pretty awesome sight. He felt like he was in the middle of a National Geographic documentary.

Emma zoomed in on the nest and snapped photo after photo of the mama bird and her chicks. Then she took out her journal and pencil and began to scribble her observations. But suddenly the point of her pencil was shaking all over the page. "Wh-what?" she sputtered.

The ground quaked beneath their feet. *It's just another tremor,* Noah thought. But a second later, a terrible rumble pounded

in his ears. It sounded like the jet engine of a 747.

"Something's wrong with the volcano!" Alex shouted. "This shouldn't be happening!"

CHAPTER 3

Noah looked toward the summit of the volcano. It seemed peaceful under the blue skies, but he turned toward his sister for reassurance anyway. "It's not going to erupt, is it?" he yelled over the roar.

"I don't know, but I'm not sticking around to find out!" Emma yelled back. "We need to head back to the boat."

"I'm with you. This is freaking me out. I've never heard anything like it before!" Alex said.

They scrambled down the mountainside as best they could, the scary-loud rumbling sound chasing after them. But it was slowgoing. Painfully slow. Running down the uneven, sloping ground was next to impossible.

"Dad said this volcano might not blow for a hundred years," Noah called out to the other two in ragged huffs. "Maybe thousands."

"In other words, it's totally unpredictable!" Emma barked back. "We can't take any chances. There's no telling how dangerous it may be!"

But Noah wasn't listening anymore. Because just then, he lost his footing on the rough terrain, fell to the ground, and slid down the slope feetfirst. His body twisted, and his stomach scraped the ground as he skidded farther down the slope. Rocks ripped at his jacket, and he clawed at everything he could to stop his momentum.

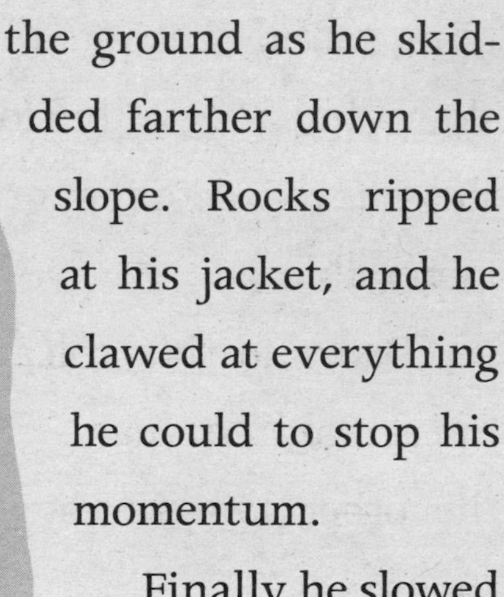

Finally he slowed enough to struggle back to his feet. He looked up the mountainside to where they'd just come from and stood paralyzed for a moment, not quite believing what he saw. "Guys! Stop! Look!" he screamed.

A deep vertical crack in the earth was cleaving the ground before his eyes. Steam and smoke sprang from the crack, which expanded quickly, snaking down toward them.

Thc other two stopped in their tracks and turned to see what Noah was screaming about.

"It's a fissure," Emma shouted. "And it'll make its way to us in a matter of seconds. We need to keep going! It could start spewing lava!"

As they hustled toward the shoreline, which still seemed impossibly far off, Noah kept glancing behind them. The fissure seemed to be catching up. It was spreading faster than they could run.

Maybe we should be running sideways to escape it, Noah thought. But by that time, they'd reached a dip in the slope that suddenly deepened and narrowed — a natural crevice that had formed years ago. They'd have to climb up a steep embankment to go sideways, which would take too much time.

"Hurry!" Alex screamed at the twins.

But Noah couldn't help craning his neck to look at the rift again. Lava was already spraying into the air where it'd first opened up. And just feet behind them, the earth continued to crack open. "It caught us!

Jump to the side! Jump to the side!" Noah bellowed.

Alex and Emma jumped to the right. Noah jumped to the left. In an instant they were separated by the fissure, which had split the earth between them.

They couldn't continue the way they'd been going. The crack was too close. And there was no telling when lava and gases would come pouring out of it.

Noah watched as Alex, in a move like Spider-Man, climbed up the steep incline on his side of the crevice. He waited at the top for Emma to follow. But Emma was tiny and not athletic at all. She kept slipping as she tried to claw her way up. Noah watched helplessly as Alex knelt down with his hand extended, trying to pull Emma up. But she couldn't reach his hand.

Steam started to rise from the opening, and Noah knew his best chance to reach the shoreline was to climb up his side of the crevice and get as far away as possible. Still, he remained frozen in place, watching his sister struggle.

Emma spun around and looked at him. "Go," she shrieked. "Just go. Don't worry about me."

By now molten lava gushed from all along the fissure, a glowing serpent racing toward them. But Noah couldn't leave Emma behind. He wouldn't. On instinct, he got a running start and leapt over the deep split in the earth that held a cauldron of boiling lava. Lava ready to spew up and incinerate anything in its way . . .

CHAPTER 4

As Noah landed his giant leap, he heard an ominous hiss and felt a warning wave of heat at his back. He wrapped his arms around Emma and lifted her toward Alex's outstretched hand.

"Almost. Just another inch!" Alex yelled.

Noah strained and grunted until Alex finally got a good grip on her hand. Alex pulled as Emma dug into the earth with her feet, desperately trying to get some traction. The next few seconds seemed to last forever, but eventually she managed to clamber up the side of the crevice, and Noah scurried up after her.

They'd made it just in time. Lava violently shot up from the opening, splattering all around them like a fiery orange hailstorm. Poisonous gases began to fill the air, and they coughed and sputtered but wasted no time stumbling over the rugged terrain away from the lava and its venomous show of force.

Noah had seen lava at Kilauea plenty of times before, but it'd been nothing like this! Visitors were always kept a safe distance away from the stable eruptions. His dad was one of the select few allowed past the barriers. Sometimes he'd even don a fireproof suit and collect lava from trails that oozed at a snail's pace. But even his dad wouldn't mess around with a fast-moving fissure like the one they'd just escaped!

With pounding hearts driving them onward, the kids ran at full speed until Emma stopped to catch her breath a good fifteen minutes later. She bent over, hands on her knees. "We should be safe now," she panted. "Fissures aren't as explosive as when the summit blows. We should be far enough away now to be okay."

As Emma talked, Noah noticed his arm was stinging. The front of his jacket had ripped when he fell, and now it had a quarter-sized burn on the sleeve. A blob of lava must have singed its way through the jacket. His shirt sleeve was intact, but the intensity of the heat still managed to burn his arm. It hurt, but he knew it could've been much worse. Silly with relief, he couldn't help but crack a joke. "First time I've worn this jacket. Ruined already."

"Yeah, wait until Dad sees it. You're going to get in so much trouble!" Emma played along. She'd finally caught her breath, and now she stood up straight. "Thanks, Noah." She walked over and hugged her twin.

They bickered a lot, being so different, so it was something she didn't do often and it caught Noah off guard.

"It was truly stupid of you to try to rescue me, but I'm awful glad you did," she said.

Noah grinned and hugged her back. He was glad, too. He couldn't have lived with himself if he'd left her.

"Thanks for pulling me up, too, Alex," Emma said, pulling away from her brother. "You're brave. You could've left us both in the dust. And I'd be toast right about now."

The volcano's rumbling seemed quieter . . . for now. "We should probably go down to the boat and meet up with Dad," Noah said, looking around. He frowned. "But which way do we go to get back to the boat?"

Emma crooked her neck in both directions, and Noah grew concerned. What if they were lost? Dad was probably already waiting for them and he'd be worried.

"We ran straight down from the eagle's nest, then veered to the right when the fissure caught up to us." Alex took his compass out of his pocket and looked at it, then squinted toward the coastline in the distance. "If we head down from here, I think we should be near the boat."

Suddenly the volcano's constant grumbling grew louder. The earth shook once again, with much more force than before. But before Noah could wrap his mind around what was happening —

BOOM!

An ear-shattering explosion rocked the earth and blackened the sky.

CHAPTER 5

The bright sunshine disappeared. Instinctively Noah looked toward the top of the mountain. Instead of the usual trail of white puffy smoke coming from the summit, a dark expanding mushroom-shaped ash cloud loomed overhead.

For a second, Noah, Emma, and Alex remained still, spellbound at the sight.

Then a large smoldering chunk of rock

came hurtling toward them, landing with a loud crash only feet away from where they were standing.

Emma screamed. "That could have hit us!"

"We need to get out of here!" Noah urged. "Right now!"

"But where?" Emma looked at Noah, her eyes desperate. "There's nowhere to go!"

Bits and pieces of what was once the top of the inside of the crater began to rain down on them.

"Over here!" Alex called. "Quick!"

Noah and Emma followed him, holding their hands over their heads to protect themselves from falling debris.

Alex led them to a small cave similar to the one Noah had peeked inside earlier.

The opening of this one was narrow, with room for only one person to crawl inside at a time.

Alex shooed Emma inside first and waited for Noah to follow her before scuttling in himself.

Past the small opening, the cave widened. It was about five feet high, ten feet wide, and not deep at all. The kids huddled on the cold, damp ground and listened to the sky falling outside. Noah knew there was nothing to do but get used to their new surroundings. Only he didn't like the thought of being stuck in the cave. He was starting to feel claustrophobic.

"So how long do we stay in here? Are we safe?" Noah asked Emma. For once he was glad his sister was a know-it-all. She always took an interest in the science of volcanoes, just like their dad, so out of the three of them he figured that made her the expert.

In the dimness of the small cave, Emma pushed at the bent plastic frames of her glasses, trying to straighten them without much success. "Safer than being outside," Emma said. "We need to stay put until the rocks from the blast stop falling. But we can't stay here for long. Flows of lava could be headed our way. Or worse, a sudden mudslide."

Noah shuddered at the thought of being entombed by lava or mud. Sealed up for eternity, never to be found. It didn't help his feeling of claustrophobia. "I hate volcanoes," he said. "They're terrible."

Even in the scenario they found themselves in, Emma couldn't resist. "That's true. But they're also responsible for creating eighty percent of the land in the world. There would be no Hawaii if it weren't for volcanoes erupting," Emma said. "And they make the soil rich for farming. So there's a bright side."

Before Noah could get exasperated at her, Alex exclaimed, "A bright side for us? Right now?"

"Nope. For us, volcanoes stink. Big-time," she admitted. After that, there was nothing much left to say, and the kids settled into an uncomfortable silence.

After a while, the chatter of falling rocks seemed to fade. When Noah peeked through the opening of the cave, he saw only delicate ash drifting down like a gentle snowfall.

"I think it's time to get going," Alex said. He started for the opening, but Emma grabbed him. "Wait."

"Why?" Noah asked. He was anxious to get out of the cramped cave, too.

"It's dangerous to breathe in the ash that's coming down," she said.

"Yeah, but it's better than being buried alive in here," Noah replied. "You were the one who mentioned lava flows and mudslides."

"I know. Just give me a minute and we can go." She opened her backpack and took out a bottle of water.

Noah was thirsty, too, but this was no time for a water break. They needed to get back to the boat while they had the chance. "A drink can wait! Let's go!" he said impatiently.

"You both need to unzip your jackets," she said. "Pour some water down the front of your shirt and pull it up so it covers your mouth and nose. Sort of like a mask."

Just as Noah was about to do as he was told, something smashed into the cave and shook its foundations. The abrupt noise startled Noah so much he leapt up, almost hitting his head on the low ceiling.

When he looked over, his heart sank. A boulder had rolled down the volcano slope and settled itself in front of the cave opening . . . blocking their only way out.

CHAPTER 6

A ray of subdued light streamed in over the top of the huge rock.

"You think there's enough room to climb over it?" Alex asked.

"I sure hope so," Noah said. He tried to squelch the panicky feeling that was tightening inside his throat. Losing it wouldn't help anything.

"You're the smallest, Emma," Alex said. "You go first."

Emma splashed her T-shirt with some water and dropped the bottle and her backpack on the ground. "One of you can hand me my backpack when I get out," she told them. "Remember to dampen your shirts, too, before you leave this cave."

She leaned over the boulder and discovered that she was barely tall enough to stick her head out of the opening. The boys lifted her as she scrunched and inched her way through the hole. Carefully, she

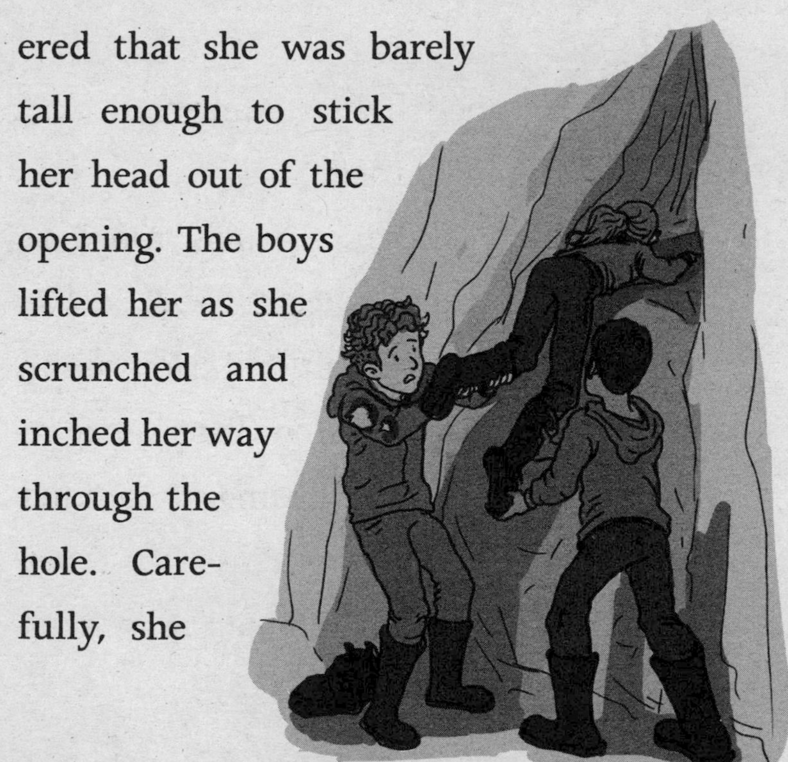

twisted her body until she was sitting on top of the boulder and dropped to the ground.

Noah tossed her backpack to her, then he and Alex doused their shirts.

"Next!" Noah heard Emma's muffled call through the wet shirt she held over her mouth and nose.

"Go ahead," Alex told Noah.

"You sure?" he asked.

"We don't have time to argue or be polite. Just move!" Alex ordered. His voice was firm, but he was smiling in encouragement.

Noah did as he was told. He was taller than Emma, so he was able to stick one shoulder and his head through the opening while still standing on the ground. The air outside was thick with floating ash, and he held his breath as he planted his hands near the top of the huge rock and dug the toes of his boots into the boulder. He wiggled, pulling himself up, bit by bit.

It was a tight squeeze. He was much thicker than Emma, and for a moment he thought he might be stuck. *Sort of like Winnie-the-Pooh wedged in Rabbit's hole,* he thought. If his life hadn't depended on getting out, he might have found the situation amusing. He could feel Alex shoving him from behind. After a struggle that left him red in the face, he finally scrunched the rest of the way out and scrambled down to join his sister. He quickly pulled up his shirt and popped the hood of his jacket over his head to keep the ash out.

It wasn't long before everyone realized that Alex couldn't make it out like the Burton twins had. For one thing, he was stockier than Noah, and Noah had barely made it through the tight opening. Plus Alex had no one left to help push him from behind.

Noah could just make out Alex's grimace. His new friend's eyes were panicked as he tried to force himself through the narrow space. He'd gotten his head and arms out, but the rest of him remained stubbornly stuck. Emma and Noah grabbed his hands and pulled, but he didn't budge.

Finally Alex waved them off dejectedly. "It's no use," he said. "Leave me here. Meet up with your dad, and go back to get help."

Noah glanced around. He saw only the fiery orange lava flow to the west where the fissure had spouted, and nothing coming toward them from farther up the slope. But that didn't mean the cave was out of harm's way. It'd take hours to get help. Who knew what could happen in that time? Lava could start pouring like a river from the summit's crater at any moment. Or the eruption could cause a mudslide. The cave would be swallowed up. They'd never find Alex.

"Maybe we can move the boulder out of the way," Noah suggested. The rock was sort of flattened where it met the ground but rounded everywhere else. If they could just tip it off center, it'd tumble out of the way. "You shove from the inside," he told Alcx. "Emma and I will get on either side and try to push it down the slope."

"Worth a shot." Alex slunk backward, disappearing inside the cave. "Tell me when you're ready!"

Noah noticed Emma was beginning to look like a gray soot-colored ghost. And his own eyelashes were caked with ash. He resisted the urge to brush it off, knowing the effort was futile. Everything seemed so harrowing and surreal. All at once, he decided he could take living away from Hawaii for a year. It didn't seem like such a big deal anymore. He just wanted them all to escape with their lives. So instead of focusing on the ash that would fall no matter what he did, he showed Emma the best place to grab hold of the boulder.

"Whatever you do," he told her, "stand clear. Wedge yourself as close to the side of the cave as possible, but don't get in front of it. If we knock the boulder loose, it's going to flatten anything in its path."

"I think I have that figured out," she answered sarcastically.

He got on the other side of the boulder. "Alex, get ready. On the count of three!" he shouted. "One . . . two . . ." Noah took a breath and dropped his shirt from his face. "Three!"

The boulder rocked forward an inch or two. Noah leaned his shoulder in. He dug his feet into the ash-covered ground. It felt slippery, like a freshly watered lawn. He turned the sole of his boot sideways and pushed with every bit of strength he had. Suddenly the boulder broke loose and went tumbling down the volcano's slope.

And there was Alex, standing just inside the cave, a look of triumph spreading across his face. But there was no time for celebratory high fives. They needed to get going!

Lightning flashed overhead. A clap of thunder broke their awed silence, and rain began to pelt them from above.

"You've got to be kidding me," Noah

said. "It wasn't supposed to rain today. Like we need this on top of everything else."

"The weatherman didn't know the volcano would erupt," Emma said matter-of-factly. "Blasts like this one often create storms. The ash particles and warmer turbulent air generate static electricity."

"Can you give us the science lesson later, Emma?" Noah said. "We've got to escape this island of doom. The sooner the better!"

The three began the slog down to the shoreline. Though the sun wouldn't set for some time, the storm and ash had darkened the skies. Except for the bright bolts of lightning, it was hard to see exactly where they were going, so Alex took out his compass and led the way.

Noah thought about his father. Dr. Burton had taken off in the opposite direction when he, Emma, and Alex had headed for the eagle's nest. So he wouldn't have been anywhere near the fissure. But what about the molten rock that had exploded out of the crater? Alex had found a safe place for them in the cave, but his father might not have been so lucky.

"Do you think Dad is okay?" Noah asked.

"He studies volcanoes for a living," Emma answered. Her voice was firm and determined, but she didn't elaborate further.

And deep down, Noah knew why. Emma was smart, but his question was one that she couldn't answer.

CHAPTER 7

As the kids made their way down the treacherous slope, the rain eventually eased, but the ash was ever present. They only paused briefly every once in a while to dampen their shirts to breathe through, and then they trudged onward. Noah tried to take his mind off his worries about his father by asking Alex what life was like in his isolated town. "There are only a few hundred people where you live and no easy way to travel anywhere else. Do you ever feel stuck?" he asked. "Bored?"

"Nah," Alex said. "I'm surrounded by wide-open spaces. If you look beyond the abandoned buildings, there's a lot of beauty. It's home. I keep busy. I have school and homework like anyone else. Sometimes I help my dad and the fishing crew on the big boat. I hang out a lot with my friend Ryan. You'll have to meet him soon. We play video games and soccer. Sometimes we go exploring. There's lots to explore. The lagoon. The bays. The waterfalls. I think I've got a pretty nice life."

"Do you ever play baseball?" Noah asked.

"Sure. I've got a decent arm, and Ryan's pretty impressive with the bat."

"I brought my mitt," Noah said. "Maybe we can play sometime."

"Are there any girls my age on the island?" Emma asked.

"A few. I think you'll especially like Julia. She gets straight As and loves going to the lagoon to watch the sea otters and seals. McKenzie, not so much. She's boy crazy and always pestering me!" He laughed and nudged Noah. "Maybe she'll meet you and finally leave me alone!"

Noah thought the kids he described seemed pretty much like the kids he knew back in Hawaii. Maybe life in Alaska wouldn't be so bad after all. At least it wouldn't once they found his dad.

As they continued down the slope, the ground went from hard and rocky to soft, moss-covered tundra, and with each step, Noah sunk into the mushy ground. He felt damp, dirty, and exhausted. He couldn't wait to get back to the duplex and take a shower, change into some clean clothes, and collapse.

"How much longer, do you think, until we get back to the bo —" Noah's foot suddenly slipped and his stomach lurched as he fell through into an abyss. He didn't realize what had happened until he lay sprawled at the bottom of a hole.

"Noah!" he heard Emma scream.

"Where'd he go, Alex? How could he just vanish?"

"Down here," Noah called.

Alex's shadow appeared overhead. Then suddenly Emma was on her hands and knees looking down at him, too.

"A sinkhole," Alex said. "Sometimes moss grows over them. You don't know they're there until it's too late. I've fallen into a few myself over the years. You okay?"

Noah struggled to his feet. The hole was a little deeper than he was tall. His thick pants had ripped, exposing a bleeding knee. His left wrist hurt, too. He tried to move it and winced. He forgot about covering his mouth with his shirt and sucked in a mouthful of ash. Sputtering, he quickly pulled his shirt over his nose with his good arm. "Yeah. Just banged up, I think. Especially my wrist. Don't know. Might be broken — but it's not like there are any bones sticking out at least."

"Can you climb out?" Alex asked.

Noah took a deep breath, dropped his T-shirt, and tried to pull himself up, but the hole was earthy and damp, and his boots kept slipping.

Alex grabbed hold of his good wrist and pulled, but it didn't seem to help. Emma's eyes darted back and forth between Noah and the volcano's summit, her face tensed in an unreadable mask.

A loud clamor thundered in the distance. It reminded Noah of the rolling, crashing waves he loved to surf. But instead of pleasure, the sound filled him with dread.

"Mudslide!" Emma shouted. "I can't see it, but I can hear it!"

Before Noah could react, Emma jumped to her feet. He thought she was about to run, but she reached down and grabbed his bad wrist with both her hands. The pain was excruciating. Noah let out a yelp, but he didn't pull away. Alex still clung to his other wrist, and both he and Emma were pulling with all their might. The tip of Noah's boot hit a jut in the earth and he strained, trying to help hoist his own body upward.

All the while the din of the mudslide grew louder.

CHAPTER 8

Noah felt his body pop out of the hole, like a jack-in-the-box springing to life. He scrambled to his feet. There was no time to think. Which way should they run?

Emma pulled at him frantically as the crashing became ear-shattering. "I can see it coming! Come on!"

Noah looked over his shoulder. The mudslide was a dark stream toppling everything in its path, including the glowing fissure to the west. The ravenous mud quickly extinguished the spraying lava as it rushed down the slope.

Would it reach them? They weren't about to wait to find out.

With their sights set on the shoreline, the three kids ran as fast as their legs would carry them. They swung their arms to gain speed and to stay balanced as their feet met the uneven ground, and as a result they couldn't cover their mouths. Noah inhaled particles of ash, but despite the gritty taste and choking sensation, he raced on.

He didn't dare take another peek behind him, but he knew the mudslide was about

to overtake them. He felt it, heard it. Out of the corner of his eye, Noah saw the worst thing possible. Emma couldn't control her speed and fell. But before he could react, his footing slipped, the ground beneath him turning from solid mush to total sludge. His body met mud. It splattered on his face, it consumed his legs. He lifted himself — despite the stabbing pain shooting through his injured wrist — and raised his head as high as he could. Now all he could do was wait for the onslaught to envelop him. Had it already buried Emma? Alex?

The crashing roar echoed as the mudslide continued its rampage all the way to the shoreline, which Noah could now make out through the haze of ash. The deluge spilled into the ocean, dancing with the waves in a riotous duel.

Somehow Noah had missed the worst of it. They'd been caught by only the very edge of the mudslide. "Emma?" he called. He craned his head behind him, looking for his sister. He saw her backpack, resting on her back like a polka-dotted turtle shell, but he couldn't see the rest of her. "Emma!" he shouted.

Noah desperately tried to pull his legs free from the gluey mud blanketing the lower portion of his body. A sock-covered foot pulled loose, but his boot remained stuck.

Luckily, when he looked back up, Emma's head had peeked out from the grimy mess. She struggled to sit up and tried to wipe at least some of the mud from her face and eyes. She took a gulp of air and coughed. "N-Noah," she sputtered. "Thank goodness you're okay. Where's Alex?"

Noah had lost sight of him as they tried to outrun the mudslide. He studied the landscape, his eyes straining to spot any movement or the flash of blue from Alex's jacket.

But all he saw was mud. Dirty, sticky, lifeless mud.

CHAPTER 9

Just then Noah heard something. It sounded like someone was hacking up a lung. He turned and spotted Alex, who must have outrun the edge of the mudslide altogether. He was bent over, his hands on his knees as he heaved and spit out a mouthful of ash. He paused and looked up at Noah and Emma, a relieved smile flashing across his face at the sight of them, before re-covering his mouth and nose with his T-shirt.

Noah dug his boot out of the mud and struggled to get it back on. His sock was covered in wet gook, which felt weird and uncomfortable, but he didn't care. That was the least of his worries. He coughed up a bunch of ash himself and covered his lower face with his shirt.

Noah and Alex carefully made their way toward Emma through the almost knee-high mud. The muck sucked at their boots with every step, threatening to pull them off, but eventually they reached Emma and helped yank her loose from the mud's sticky embrace. After some more slogging they were once again on solid ground, where they picked up the pace to reach the shoreline.

"You don't think the mudslide got the boat do you?" Noah asked.

"I don't know. If it missed the boat, it didn't miss it by much," Alex said. "I lost my compass somewhere in the rush of the mudslide, but now that we're getting closer, I don't really need it. Let's just follow the edge of the mudslide. Hopefully we'll see it just a bit farther down the coastline."

Though the rain had stopped earlier, a stray bolt of lightning flashed, illuminating what a sorry sight they were. The mud coating Noah's body had begun to stiffen. He felt filthy and cold. His wrist ached. All he wanted was to see his father again. And go back to the duplex. He imagined what it would feel like to be washed clean in a warm shower and then to fall into a cozy bed. Grandma Tilda was waiting for them. She must have heard the volcano blast and saw the thick smoke rising from it. She must be worried sick about them. Noah hoped he'd get to see her soon and reassure her that they were truly okay.

They'd almost made it to the shore when Emma started to cry. She was trying to hide it, but Noah could hear her sniffling and saw her shoulders shake.

He crept closer to her and put his arm around her.

"What if Dad was on the boat waiting

for us?" she managed to eke out between sniffles. "And it got caught up in the mudslide?"

Noah had been wondering the same thing. His own throat grew tight and this time it was not because of the ashen air.

"Guys, look!" Alex suddenly screamed, pointing.

Not even a hundred yards from the mud-covered outcropping where the beach met the ocean, a white boat bobbed in the waves, right where it had been anchored and left.

Never had Noah been so happy to see a boat before. It offered escape from this nightmare of an island. And hopefully a familiar face waiting for them.

"Dad!" Emma called out as they ran toward the boat. "Dad!"

There was no answer.

Noah ran across the outcropping and jumped into the air, landing soundly on deck. He peeked inside the small cabin. It was empty.

"Dad's not here." Crushed, he turned to

the other two, who were still standing on the rocky outcropping beside the boat.

"Maybe he's looking for us," Emma said. "I hope . . . I hope he went looking for us after the mudslide. Not before . . ." Her voice trailed off. "Maybe we should go looking for him?"

"No," Alex said firmly. "We need to stay put. If we go looking for him, he might circle back and we'd miss each other. Let's wait for him. We can take off when he shows up. Okay?"

Emma nodded. Noah thought her eyes looked sadder than he'd ever seen them. He stretched out his good hand and helped Emma maneuver onto the boat as it jostled in the waves. Alex quickly followed.

They shook off as much ash as they could and hurried inside the cabin, where they could breathe without inhaling the toxic air. Emma grabbed bottles of water from the cooler to soothe their dry, gritty throats.

There was a small spot on the cabin's window not covered in soot and Emma peered out it intently. Noah knew she was hoping to catch their father's tall figure approaching through the falling ash.

How long can we stay here? Noah wondered. Alex must be anxious to get back home — back to where it was safe and he could be reunited with his parents.

Noah gave him an appreciative look. "Thanks," he said.

"For what?" Alex asked. "I didn't do anything special. We all played a part in getting back to the boat alive."

"I mean, thanks for not wanting to start up the motor and get the heck out of here without waiting to see if our dad comes back."

Alex shrugged it off. "If it were my dad, I'd want to wait for him, too."

The kids waited anxiously as afternoon turned into evening. The skies, already dark with ash, blackened as night fell on the island.

Noah's stomach grumbled.

"We should eat a little something," Emma said. "But not too much. Just in case . . ."

"In case we're here for a while," Alex finished for her.

They ate some of the food Dr. Burton had packed in the cooler for the trip home, each taking a slice of cheese and a slice of bread, but resisting the urge to plow into the rest of the feast. The air was cold, but they were out of the wind and their muddy clothes had finally dried out.

"I've got an idea," Alex said, after he quickly polished off his small dinner. "Let's set off one of the emergency flares. I don't know why I didn't think of it sooner. My dad always keeps them on his boats. If your dad is searching for us, he'll see it and know we're back here in the boat."

Alex quickly found a flare and set it off. The kids watched it streak into the sky and then explode in a red burst. Hopefully Dr. Burton would see it through the ash.

Twenty minutes later, though he willed them not to, Noah's eyes began to droop. He was bone tired. But just as he was drifting off to sleep, he heard the sound of a boat horn in the distance and his eyes flew open.

"It's my dad's other boat. The big one." Alex jumped up and looked out the cabin door to see if he could catch sight of it. "He's coming for us. I know it's him! I'm sure he was frantic when the volcano erupted and we didn't return."

The boat's VHF radio crackled. A voice asked for confirmation. Alex answered with the boat's name and switched the channel so he could talk to his dad directly.

"Alex! Thank God you are all right!" Mr. Kozloff's relieved voice came over the handheld speaker.

"Yes, I'm on the boat with Emma and Noah. But Dr. Burton is missing," Alex told him.

Noah wondered if that meant that Mr.

Kozloff would force him and Emma to go back with him. *I can't,* he thought. *I can't just leave without him.* He wasn't ready to give up on his father just yet.

As it turned out, he didn't have to. In what little moonlight there was, Noah saw a familiar lanky figure climb aboard the boat.

"Dad!" he cried. He and Emma lunged toward their father, practically knocking him off his feet as they jumped into his outstretched arms.

"You're okay! You're really okay! I can't believe it!" Dr. Burton, hysterical with laughter and tears, kissed each of his children. "I searched and searched for you. I thought . . ." He paused, the idea too awful to continue. He clung to both of them tightly.

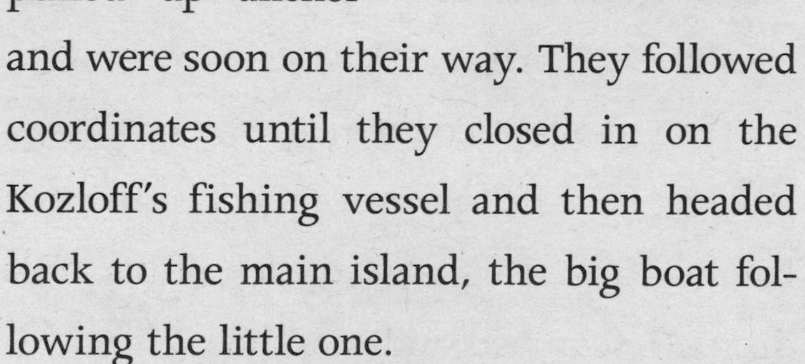

After the hurried reunion, Dr. Burton spoke on the radio with Alex's father and then quickly started up the boat's engine. When it had sputtered to life, they pulled up anchor and were soon on their way. They followed coordinates until they closed in on the Kozloff's fishing vessel and then headed back to the main island, the big boat following the little one.

Noah glanced back at the volcano. The

peak glowed orange in the moonlight, and lava was beginning to ooze from its mouth. He wondered if the volcano was done with them. Or if it was just getting started . . .

CHAPTER 10

It was the first clear day Noah had seen since the volcano erupted. For almost two weeks, a light dusting of ash drifted over to their small island town, coating nearly everything powdery gray. But the volcano was finally still. It'd had its say, and now it was done with its tantrum.

Noah and Emma had mostly stayed inside during the past weeks, but they hadn't been bored for a second of it. Since their father was a well-known volcanologist, their duplex became command central for the town. In the days following the blast, their little apartment hosted a constant stream of media reporters and other visiting scientists. But today, with the sun peeking through the clouds and the air finally clean, Noah was anxious to get out and explore his new surroundings. He and Emma, along with Alex and his friends Julia and Ryan, were planning to hike to a nearby lagoon for the afternoon.

Alex showed up at their door with a tall boy in a gray sweatshirt and a girl sporting long hair and a purple jacket. Introductions were made, and soon the small gang of kids was on its way, walking the three miles to the lagoon by way of an old, pock-marked road with virtually no traffic.

Noah filled his lungs with a deep breath of air. It sure felt good to be able to breathe without a shirt for a mask! His wrist was feeling much better, too. Fortunately it had only been a sprain.

Emma wore her binoculars around her neck, ready to spy on any creatures that happened to cross their path. "I really hope we get to see some sea otters. And sea lions," she said.

"The sea otters are my favorite. They're hilarious!" Julia said. "They like to pester each other when they play. They remind me of little kids." She grinned. "Sort of like Ryan and Alex when they get carried away."

"Hey, who're you calling a little kid? I'm almost a year older than you!" Alex nudged her, laughing.

"Yeah, but you guys do act like little kids sometimes. Girls are way more mature, you know," she teased.

"Yeah, right," Alex said, rolling his eyes.

After some more joking, the conversation took a serious turn.

"I heard the three of you were interviewed by some newspapers and a television crew," Ryan said. "About being on the island when the volcano blew. Alex told me all about it. Talk about scary! I mean, I was scared and I wasn't even that close to anything. But I sure heard, felt, and saw what was going on! I can't even imagine!"

"It *was* pretty darn scary," Noah said. "Believe me, nothing I care to ever experience again. But I guess it was kind of neat to be interviewed like that."

"The eruption attracted a lot of national attention," Emma said. "But thankfully, in the scale of things, it wasn't nearly as devastating as the eruptions at Mount St. Helens. Technically it was a significant event, but not a catastrophic one. Though it certainly felt pretty catastrophic living through it!"

Once they reached the lagoon, Emma could barely contain her excitement. There were at least twenty sea otters waiting to greet them. Some were resting on the rocky shore, while others frolicked in the water. The kids crept close enough to get a good look without disturbing them.

Emma used her binoculars to zoom in on the action, but they weren't necessary to enjoy the show some of the frisky critters

were putting on. Noah couldn't help but smile as a mother otter floated on her back while her "baby" — who was almost as big as she was — slipped on and off her belly.

"This is a really cool place," Noah said. And he meant it. Alaska was very different from Hawaii. It was rugged and wild. But Hawaii would be waiting for him when he returned. For now, he was soaking in everything Alaska had to offer. He knew, whatever the future might hold, he would forever remember this year.

After a full afternoon exploring the lagoon, Noah, Emma, and their new friends walked back to their cluster of duplexes. Julia and Emma had hit it off and had already made plans for the following day. Julia knew the perfect place to bird-watch, and they planned to fill in Emma's bird-watching journal with lots of descriptions and sketches.

As they reached the Burtons' front door, Noah turned and paused to stare at the volcano that rose across a short stretch of sea. It looked different than the day he arrived. The snow at the summit had melted, and the mudslide had turned a band of the lush green slope rough and brown. The volcano had changed. And Noah had changed, too.

"Do you guys want to come over to my house tomorrow?" Ryan asked Alex and Noah. "Maybe we can play some video games if it rains. If not, maybe we can get a baseball game going. We won't have enough for a full team, but we can practice our swings."

"Sure," Noah said. "That sounds good." And it did. Though part of him had changed, he was still ten-year-old Noah Burton.

And he was awfully glad to be alive.

More About VOLCANOES

On any given day, an average of 10–20 volcanoes around the world are spewing ash and lava. This does not include the many underwater volcanoes that exist along the ocean floor.

An active volcano is one that has erupted in the past 10,000 years. Above sea level, there are around 1,500 active volcanoes in the world. About 169 of these are located in the United States. The state with the most active volcanoes is Alaska.

Lava isn't the only thing that can erupt from a volcano. An avalanche of hot ash, pumice, rock fragments, and gas is called a pyroclastic flow. Pyroclastic flows can travel as fast as 400 miles per hour! Lava flows, on the other hand, are much slower — only about 1 to 2 miles per hour.

The biggest volcanic explosion ever recorded came from Mount Tambora, Indonesia. When it erupted in 1815, it sent so much ash into the atmosphere that it blocked out sunlight. Temperatures dropped enough that 1816 became known as "the year without summer."

The most devastating eruption in U.S. history was that of Mount St. Helens in 1980. The eruption spread ash over more than 22,000 square miles. It also caused the largest landslide ever recorded, which destroyed over 200 homes. Thankfully early warnings allowed most people to evacuate to safety.

The animals around Mount St. Helens weren't so lucky, and many died. But a group of pocket gophers survived the blast. They live deep underground in burrowed tunnels. When they surfaced after the blast, their digging brought fertile soil to the surface and mixed in seeds and plant parts. The gophers aided the eventual recovery of the area by helping wildlife to return.

Hawaii's Kilauea volcano has been erupting continuously since 1983. It is one of the world's most active volcanoes. Currently it's stable and predictable, and attracts many tourists. But in 1790, an explosive eruption killed 400 people — which is now the deadliest eruption on record in the U.S.

There are volcanoes on other planets besides Earth. The biggest volcano in our solar system is on Mars. It is about 375 miles wide and 14 miles high!

Fortunately scientists often provide advance warning when a volcano is about to erupt. It's important to follow evacuation orders promptly. If you are around when a volcano erupts without warning, there are things you can do to try to stay safe:

- Get to high ground far away from the volcano. Lava flows and mudslides move downhill, and quickly make their way to valleys and low-lying areas.
- If you are caught outside during an explosion, lay down on the ground facing away from the volcano. Protect your head from flying debris with your arms, backpack, or anything else you can find.
- If you are caught in ash fall, cover your face with a dust mask or damp cloth to avoid breathing in particles in the air, which can damage the lungs.
- If you are not in an area of immediate danger, stay inside and close all doors and windows. Since falling debris can be dangerously hot or even smoldering, watch the building for signs of fire.

Ready for another thrilling adventure?

Read on for a sneak peek at

BLIZZARD NIGHT. . .

"It'll be dark soon. And the tempera-ture has dropped. We should find shelter for the night while there's still some light left," Jayden said. "We can continue on in the morning." He flashed back to a harrowing scene in his Everest book, where a climber had almost frozen to death from hypothermia but was saved by tunneling into the snow to protect himself from the wind and trap his body heat. Here, though, the snow just wasn't deep enough yet to burrow into. Maybe they could find a hollow tree for shelter. His face already felt numb. *I could start a fire with the matches I brought,* he thought. *I bet Maggie and Connor will be glad I tagged along.* But before he could open his mouth to mention it, Maggie spoke.

"No!" she said. "W-w-we can't be that far away! In another tw-twenty minutes or so, we could be there. We should keep going."

"I agree with Maggie," Connor said. "The sun hasn't gone down yet and if we reach help soon, then by midnight Dad will have his leg in a cast and we can all spend the night in our own cabin. That's a heck of a lot better than huddling up here in the woods."

Jayden knew he was outnumbered, so he didn't argue. Plus he wanted to help their dad just as much as they did. He just hoped they were right. "So which way do we go?" he asked.

The sky was too overcast to see where

the sun was setting. There was no clue which way was north, south, east, or west.

"Let's head that way." Connor pointed. "It is to the right of our footsteps so at least we won't be going backward." He started walking, while Maggie and Jayden trailed behind.

By now Jayden was so stiff with cold that it was hard to move, but he forced each step, hoping it would take him closer to safety. And warmth. He swore he could feel the chill all the way to his bones. His cheeks began to prickle and itch, his chest ached with every breath.

They had only walked for about ten minutes when he noticed Maggie's shoulders were shaking. She was shivering badly, and had her arms wrapped around her sides. He watched as her steps grew unsteady and wobbly.

"Maggie! Are you okay?" he asked. He hurried a few steps to catch up to her.

She looked dazed. "Yeth." Then she mumbled something else, but her voice trembled and her speech was too slurred to make out.

Jayden knew she most definitely wasn't okay.

"Stop!" Jayden called out to Connor. "Hey, hold up a minute!"

"What?" Connor turned back toward Jayden and Maggie. His face was twisted in frustration, and Jayden guessed he didn't want their mission interrupted when it was so important.

"There's something wrong with Maggie," Jayden told him.

"N-n-no. N-n-n-not," Maggie said through chattering teeth. "I'm-m-m ok-k-k-kay. Let's-s-s g-g-go."

Connor gasped. "Maggie! Your lips . . . they're blue! And you're shivering like crazy!"

"We need to get her warm and find something to shelter her from the wind. Now. She looks like she might be getting hypothermia," Jayden said, trying to make his voice as firm as possible. He'd put up a fight this time if he had to. No way would he let them travel on. He remembered the hypothermia scene in his book, and it looked like Maggie had all of the same symptoms. "She's too cold! And she's losing heat faster than her body can produce it." He shook his head. "Trust me. It's dangerous!"

"Okay. But where on earth are we going to find shelter out here?" By now Connor had wrapped an arm around his sister protectively and rubbed her shoulders to help warm her.

"I'm s-s-s-sor-r-r-ry." Maggie strug gled to get the words out. "It's-s-s-s all my fault. We wil-l-l-l be s-s-s-stuck out here."

"Hush," Jayden said, cutting her off. "It's only a matter of time before Connor and I have symptoms just like yours. It's getting colder out here by the minute." The snowfall had lightened enough so that in the distance he could make out a rocky hillside. Snow had begun to drift and pile along the outcropping. "Maybe we can dig out a hole along those rocky crags over there. It looks like it's only about five minutes away."

This time he got no argument. Jayden was relieved. If he or Connor came down with hypothermia, too, there was no way they'd survive the night. Maggie hadn't shown any severe symptoms yet — like confusion, hallucinations, or acting irrationally. But he knew the three of them wandering around hopelessly lost and crazed would not end well. If they could stay warm until morning, perhaps the weather would be better for their hike to get help. Plus they'd be able to see the sun rise so they could get a sense of which direction to go.

With Maggie in the middle, and the boys hovering on either side of her to keep the wind and cold at bay, the group made their way through the woods to the rocky hillside.

When they came within feet of the area, Connor grew excited. "Hey, look, isn't that a cave?"

Jayden spotted the darkened hole in the hillside. They wouldn't have to dig a tunnel through snow to make shelter. A safe place out of the wind and snow was right there waiting for them!

"It's a cave! It is!" Jayden could hardly

believe their good fortune. The cave looked to be about four feet high and about the same wide, but the wind had created a snowdrift near the entrance that would need to be cleared. He could probably kick a path through it for them in a matter of minutes. "Hold on to Maggie," Jayden told Connor, "while I get the snow out of the way."

Though he felt stiff and achy, the excitement of knowing something Maggie and Connor didn't spurred him on. He had the book of matches in his pocket! Soon they'd be sitting near a fire. Thank goodness he thought to bring them after all! He quickly set to work shoving aside about two feet of drifted snow. Once done, he stooped over and made his way inside the cave, waving for Connor and Maggie to follow him. It was dim inside, but it looked plenty deep enough for the three of them to cozy up. He was in such a hurry to get Maggie inside that he didn't notice the dip in the ground until it was too late.

As he fell, he reached out with his gloved hands to catch himself. But the landing wasn't as hard as he'd expected. In fact, it was kind of soft. And surprisingly warm. His face brushed up against something furry, and he froze in shock.

The soft lump he landed on stirred.

Jayden's first instinct was to scream and

run. It took all the strength he could muster to remain still. A scene from a book he'd read nearly a year ago came flooding back to him. A boy had accompanied his father, a zoologist, on a trip to study caribou in the Alaskan wilderness. The boy wandered off and eventually came upon an angry mama bear. He knew not to run and it saved his life. There is no way to outrun a bear. They're faster, hands down. And running makes the bear think you're prey.

Slowly and quietly, Jayden eased his way up to his feet. He didn't want to rouse the bear. With luck it would drift back into its winter slumber, totally unaware that its space had been invaded.

"Holy cow!" Connor gasped from behind when he noticed the large creature inhabiting the cave. "Run!" He spun around and reached for his sister's hand so he could drag her along in his attempt to escape.

Jayden grabbed Connor by the arm, twisting him back before he could flee. "Don't!" He looked at Connor as gravely as possible and spoke in a low, soft voice. "He'll go after you and he'll win."

Just then, the bear emitted a low grumbling moan and lumbered to its feet, sniffing the air and pawing the ground. Connor looked unsure about the advice Jayden had just given him, but did as he was told.

"Back away slowly," Jayden whispered. "And whatever you do, don't look him in the eye."

Maggie seemed awestruck by the majestic beast. She took a staggering step forward toward the bear. *She doesn't know any better,* Jayden thought. *The hypothermia is getting to her. She's totally out of it.*

Connor, realizing his sister was not to be trusted in her current state, scooped her up into his arms and slowly began to inch backward. Jayden followed as quietly as he could. He kept his eyes firmly on the ground. Slowly but surely the three kids made their way out of the cave.

At first it appeared the bear might remain inside. But then it, too, cautiously emerged from the cave and approached them. Fear poured through Jayden. He stared at the huge clawed paws that padded the snow-covered ground. He tried not to think of the damage they could do.

"I think we should play dead," Connor whispered, his voice barely loud enough to be heard.

Jayden remembered that the boy from his book had tried that, and the bear had left him alone. But later, the boy's father had told him how lucky he was that it was a grizzly bear he'd met. That if it had been a hungry black bear going after him, he wouldn't have survived using that trick. And Jayden knew that grizzlies didn't live in Michigan. This one had to be a black bear. And if it decided it was hungry, they'd just make things easier for it by playing dead.

"No. Keep going. Trust me," Jayden murmured back.

The snow was deep enough to make walking backward awkward. Jayden dared a direct peek at the bear. The beast had come to a stop, and though his body remained still, he swung his head back and forth anxiously as if trying to decide what to do.

When they were about sixty feet away from the bear, Jayden breathed a sigh of relief and turned toward Maggie and Connor. "I think we're in the clear," he told them.

But he'd spoken too soon. The bear snorted. It pounded the ground. Jayden looked back just in time to catch a sudden flash of black.

The bear was charging right at them.

I SURVIVED

DO YOU HAVE WHAT IT TAKES TO SURVIVE?

READ THEM ALL, THEN TAKE THE QUIZ TO TEST YOUR SURVIVAL SKILLS AT WWW.SCHOLASTIC.COM/ISURVIVED.